MONSTER FACTORY

A Milo Jenkins Monster Hunter Thriller

PATRICK MCNULTY

A Ministry of Monsters Press

As always, this book is dedicated to my loving and devoted family and friends. Without their continued support, laughter and love my world would be a very dark place indeed.
Thank you for everything.

FOREWORD

Hi there, before you get started I just wanted to invite you to join my Advance Reader Copy Team (ARC Team) where you will have exclusive access to all the latest updates in the Ministry of Monsters universe.

Once on the list you get to read the new Milo Jenkins: Monster Hunter books before they even get released. I'm always looking for new readers, and I always listen to your suggestions and comments.

Join my ARC Team today by visiting me at: www.patrickmcnulty.ca and clicking ARC TEAM in the menu.

Three days ago in a secret underground lab beneath the town of Cripple Creek ...

"What do you mean, attack?" Dr. Stuart Devon asked the soldier on the other end of the phone.

"Exactly what I said, Doctor." The soldier replied. "The outer perimeter fence has been compromised. Until we can verify that it's just a security system malfunction, I need you and your daughter to remain in your lab."

The steely-voiced soldier sounded worried, which made Dr. Devon worried.

"Can you do that, Doc?" the soldier finished.

"Yeah," the doctor said. "Sure."

The line went dead, leaving Dr. Devon, head of the special weapons group, with a ball of ice forming in his stomach.

Attack?

Animals had run into the fence from time to time. Teenagers, feeling adventurous, had even climbed one of the perimeter fences, but Sgt. Connolly had never used the word attack before. Dr. Devon blinked and hung up the phone.

The lab was very quiet, with just the whirring of computers and the fans circulating fresh air into the room through various filters. Miles of steel-reinforced concrete and a platoon of some of the best trained and heavily armed soldiers on the planet stood between them and whatever had "compromised" the outer fence. He did a quick calculation of the odds of someone actually getting all the way down to his lab. It didn't take long. It was about a million to one. Maybe more. He turned to his daughter, letting out the breath he had been holding since Sgt. Connolly had hung up.

"Does it hurt them, Daddy?" Clare asked.

Normally, Dr. Devon would never allow his eight-year-old daughter to accompany him to his lab, but his babysitter cancelled at the last minute, and he had no other choice. Besides, he was the head of the department, and being in a super-secret underground weapons lab was probably the safest place in the world, relatively speaking.

Clare stared at the swirling black fluid inside a large clear plexiglass tower in the corner of the lab. Below the tower of swirling liquid was a clear cylinder the size of a large aquarium.

"No, no, no, darling." Dr. Devon replied. "The nanobots that make up the black sand are very tiny special computers. When they completely cover a host, they form a protective suit. You see this ring?"

Dr. Devon wriggled his fingers, letting the thick gold ring with a green cat's eye stone catch the overhead fluorescent light. "Once the suit is formed, I can use this ring to make the suit do whatever I want."

"So the person inside ..." Clare began.

" We just test the suit on animals. Since the animals tend to run away, I need to be in control to make sure the suit works."

Clare's blue eyes sparkled. She looked so much like her mom, Dr. Devon thought, so much. And, for a second, he felt like he couldn't breathe.

"Can I see one?" Clare asked. "Can I see how it works?"

Dr. Devon snuck a peek at his watch. It was getting late, but what did that matter now? They were on strict orders to remain in his lab until further notice.

"Please, Daddy."

"Honey, I don't know. It's already past your bedtime."

"Please, Daddy, I'm already in my pyjamas!"

One look at Clare's puppy dog eyes and he was defeated.

"Sure," he said.

Clare smiled, clapped her hands and wrapped her arms around her father.

"Thank you, Daddy! Thank you!"

Clare hopped off the stool at the computer station and stepped toward the north wall, which was lined with various animal cages. The clear plastic cages were stacked three high and six wide. Every enclosure was filled with a different kind of animal. Bored looking monkeys, white fluffy rabbits, tiny white mice and even hamsters.

In her fuzzy pink pajamas and matching slippers, Clare walked by each cage, her small hand stroking her smaller chin as she carefully decided. She slowed and finally stopped. Kneeling down in front of the plexiglass cage, she peered into the pile of wood shavings and pointed at the chubby little hamster inside.

"This one," she said finally.

"Perfect choice, honey."

Her dad unlocked the door and reached inside. The orange and white hamster scurried away from the doctor's hand, tunnelling through the wood shavings, making a bee-line for the back wall of his little space.

"It's all right, little guy," the doctor cooed. "It's okay."

The hamster huddled in the corner and twitched its whiskers.

Gently, he scooped up the hamster and handed him to Clare. The animal quivered in the cradle of her cupped hands.

"You're sure this won't hurt him?" Clare asked her father again. "You promise?"

"Absolutely," he replied.

Clare nuzzled the furry creature and smiled as she followed her father to the plexiglass pod. Once there, her father unlatched the pod door, and Clare was directed to place the hamster on a small metal tray. When the hamster was safely inside, he closed the pod door and secured the latch.

Clare smiled at the hamster as it sat stock still on the metal frame. She tapped the glass. On the opposite side, the chubby hamster stood up on its hind legs and placed its small paws on the glass. Its nose sniffed and twitched.

"Are you ready?" her dad asked.

Clare nodded. "Ready."

He took a seat in front of his computer and tapped a few keys.

The lab filled with the whine of a machine revving up, getting faster and faster. Clear plastic tubes connected to the main tower containing the swirling black liquid began to fill.

Clare pressed her nose to the glass and watched as the black sand covered the bottom of the pod.

The little hamster scrambled around and around on the metal tray, looking for somewhere to go, but he was trapped. He ran back to the glass and stood again on his hind legs, his whiskers twitching furiously, but it was no use. The black sand continued to pump into the clear plastic cylinder until the hamster was completely buried.

Clare turned from the plexiglass pod with tears in her eyes.

"Oh, Daddy, you've buried him!" she said. "He can't breathe!"

"He's fine, sweetheart, just watch."

The machine noise grew quiet before it stopped completely.

Clare looked back to the glass, her eyes pinned to the mound of black sand left on the metal tray. A single tear streaked down her cheek. In her heart she knew the hamster was dead, and she was to blame.

For a breathless moment, there was no movement at all.

Then the mound of black sand began to stand as if it were a snowman being made in reverse. Instead of melting into a puddle, the black sand rose, growing and forming itself into a super hamster!

The mound of sand assembled itself into shiny black dragon scales and long needle-like claws. The stylish black suit of armour molded itself around the body of the hamster.

Clare's mouth hung open.

"What is that?" she whispered.

The chubby little orange and white hamster looked like something out of the science fiction movies her dad forced her to watch some times.

"It's called a super soldier suit, for now; I haven't really come up with a better name."

"He looks like a monster."

And he did—the hamster was larger than he had been. His arms and legs were a little longer allowing his body more range of motion.

"Look at his eyes!" Clare said.

The hamster's eyes stared straight ahead with an eerie green glow.

"What can it do?"

Her dad was way ahead of her. He unlatched the pod door and scooped up the armoured hamster and carried him to his computer desk, where it remained standing at attention. He removed the gold controller ring and slipped it over his daughter's finger.

"Whoever wears the ring controls the super soldier."

Clare beamed. Her blue eyes flicked from the pretty gold ring on her finger to the armoured hamster.

"What should I have him do?"

"Anything you want."

"Run in a circle," Clare said.

Instantly, the hamster dropped to all fours and ran like mad in a circle. Clare squealed with delight.

"Stop," she commanded, and the hamster froze. "Do some jumping-jacks!"

The hamster snapped out jumping-jacks in short order, one after another and another and another.

"Oh, Daddy, I want one! I want one! My friends are gonna lose their minds! Please can I have one?"

Her dad opened his mouth, but before he could say anything, the power blinked out. The entire lab plunged into darkness.

A moment later, the emergency lighting clicked on, bathing the lab in a weird red glow.

"What's happening, Daddy?"

"I don't know, honey."

He mouthed a word. Clare wasn't sure, but it looked like *"Attack."* Her heart hammered.

It couldn't be.

She followed as her dad stepped to the sliding metal door of his lab and scanned his keycard. The lock stayed red. He swiped again. Still nothing. He moved to the lab phone and dialled. "Where are you, Sgt. Connolly?" he murmured.

Nothing.

She could hear the echo of the phone, just ringing and ringing.

Attack.

Her dad hung up the phone and fished his cell out of his pocket. He stared at the screen, but even Clare knew there was no signal down here. They were too deep. He shoved it back into his pocket and tried the other phone again.

"Who are you calling?" Clare asked.

"There should be guards out there."

Her dad waited a little and made a face before slamming it down with a crash of plastic. "Nothing but ringing."

Clare's light, quick footsteps crossed the distance to the door, and she wrapped her arms around her dad.

"Daddy, I don't like this."

"Me either," he said.

With the main power off and the door to his lab disabled, they were trapped down here. Stuck in a vault-like room ten floors below the ground. Clare turned her head as a muted click sounded. The door to the lab slid open.

She was hoping to see the grizzled face of Sgt. Connolly, or any one of her dad's men. Combat fatigues and high powered weapons at the ready. But the man who filled the doorway wasn't dressed in combat fatigues. He was dressed in a black suit and shiny black shoes.

The man's ivory skin glowed in the alien red light. He was stick thin and had to be at least seven feet tall as he ducked through the doorway. Even in the rosy gloom, he wore small round sunglasses.

The man smiled when he saw them huddled together against the wall. His smile was all wrong, filled with too many sharp crooked teeth, "Good evening, Dr. Devon."

Her dad clutched her a little tighter and stepped backward, deeper into the lab.

"Who … who are you?" he asked, in a trembling voice.

"My name is Darius Radish," the strange man said, "and I'm you're biggest fan."

Darius glided into the lab followed by a small team of soldiers dressed from head to toe in black camouflage. They were squat and powerful and heavily armed. Clare's dad pushed her behind him.

"This is a secure facility," he said, watching Darius step toward his computer station. The hamster Clare had ordered to snap out jumping jacks was still cracking them out one after another like a machine.

"You can't be here," Stuart continued. "This is a military installation."

Darius bent down until he was face to face with the jumping jack hamster.

"I'm well aware, Doctor," he said. "I saw the marines on the way in." He directed his eyes to the hamster. "Cute," he hissed. "Where's the ring?"

Clare moved even further behind her dad, but not before Darius caught sight of her, covering the ring with her palm.

He moved so fast Clare could scarcely detect it. One second he was on the opposite side of the room staring at the hamster, and then, with a puff of foul smelling breath, his skeletal face was inches from Clare's own.

He removed his sunglasses, and Clare could see that his eyes were entirely red, the orange light inside his eye sockets crackled and swayed like firelight.

"You're a brave one, I can tell," he said.

He opened his enormous right hand, unfolding a set of fingers that held too many knuckles. He held his hand out, palm up in front of the little girl.

"The ring please."

Clare slipped the controller ring from her finger and placed it carefully into the man's giant hand. His long, double jointed fingers snapped closed around it like a bear trap, and when he stood to his full height Clare saw that he had slipped the ring onto one of his extra-long fingers.

Darius smiled his awful scary smile. As he stared lovingly at the ring he whispered, "This is going to be fun."

Wychwood Academy

CHAPTER ONE

"Milo! Wake up!"

Toby's voice cut through my brain like a buzz saw. I was having such an awesome dream. Running on the sand with Floyd, the sun on my shoulders, the warm sand between my toes, ocean waves crashing into the pearly white sand, and then—

"Milo!"

I blinked into the daylight. Floyd, my Jack Russell terrier, stared at me from across the pillow. I had been away for the last three days on a mission for Ministry of Monsters (MOM), and I think the little guy had been missing me.

"Enough is enough!" Toby whined. "I can't take it anymore! You are such a slob."

"I think he's talking about you," I whispered to Floyd.

Floyd responded with a loud yawn followed by a squeaky fart.

He wasn't a big fan of Toby, and the feeling was mutual.

"Do you see this?" Toby said. He had something clutched in his pale fist as he stomped across the duct tape line he had placed down the centre of our shared room. Toby was dressed for the day in the Wychwood Academy uniform. His downy white shirt practically gleamed and you could cut yourself on the creases in his pants.

His side of the room practically gleamed; everything was stored in its proper place, everything was squared away. Mine, well, I'm not gonna lie. Cleaning my room was neither my highest priority, nor my strong suit, and it showed.

Toby had to tiptoe in his shiny black shoes around piles of dirty clothes, empty take out containers from the cafeteria and mounds of discarded books to even get close to my bed.

This year, Toby and I both turned thirteen, which meant we had graduated from the junior barracks to the senior rooms where we went from sharing a room with five other students, to sharing a room with just one.

"It's bad enough that the dean allows you keep that *animal* in our room."

Floyd lifted his head from the pillow and glanced at

Toby. It was like he knew he was talking about him, and he probably did; Floyd was a pretty smart dog.

"But this," he said, holding out his clutched fist, "I will not tolerate."

I sat up in bed as he opened his hand and let the remains of what looked like confetti flutter into my lap.

"I've told you a million times to stay on your side of the room and not to allow any of your trash to cross the line."

"How do you know they're mine?"

Toby snorted. "These are candy wrappers, and I don't poison my body with sugar. There's only the two of us in here, so you figure it out."

Toby's usually pale face was turning darker red by the second with a finger-thick vein pulsing in time with his racing heart in the centre of his forehead.

Floyd yawned again and lifted his head from my pillow. He stepped over to the pile of plastic confetti and began rooting around, sniffing and licking the bigger pieces.

Toby watched Floyd with a twisted look of naked disgust on his face.

"I'm serious, Milo," he said. "I find more of your garbage on my side of the room, and I'm going to the dean."

Toby checked his watch.

"Last warning, Milo." He turned on his heel and stormed out of our room.

Floyd found something worth licking on one of the pieces of candy wrappers, and it got stuck to the end of his nose. He looked funny as he first tried to remove the wrapper with his tongue, then his front paws, and finally by driving his snout into my comforter in an attempt to scrape it off.

In the end, he whined and begged me to help.

The shredded wrapper was from a Nutty Buddy and, as I was gathering up the other bits scattered on my bed, I noticed the tiny little teeth marks. Really tiny teeth marks. I picked up several other pieces and looked at them more closely.

These were goblin teeth marks.

CHAPTER TWO

My name is Milo Jenkins. I'm thirteen, live here at the Wychwood Academy and I hunt monsters.

Also, I'm not a big fan of goblins. If you've never seen one, picture a slimy, jellyfish rat that's as big as a fifth grader and loves eating anything that's not locked down. I had a sinking feeling in my stomach when I saw the shredded candy wrappers. I think I knew where they came from, but I was hoping I was wrong.

I slipped out of bed, and Floyd followed me, looking puzzled.

The closet door was left open, as usual, with a pair of my gym shorts and one nasty smelling sneaker jamming the door open. I ripped the closet door wide open and peered inside.

"NOOOOOOO!"

It felt like my heart was breaking. Inside the closet on the mound of clothes were the remains of my enchanted Halloween bag. I fell to my knees and cradled the shredded bag in my hands. Tiny teeth marks had ripped through the lining, tearing it completely to shreds. I'd gotten it after capturing a witch who'd been on the loose in Toronto, Canada. Pale blue with a shiny silver fringe, it was smaller than a pillow case and had been spellbound to never get full or heavy, no matter how much candy I dropped into it. But now it was gone. All my Nutty Buddy's, all my Twisty Goos, everything.

All gone.

The temperature in my bedroom dropped sharply, and Floyd barked. He did that whenever a ghost came into my bedroom, even though I'd told him a thousand times, "It's just Ruby, Floyd."

Ruby Sinclair was a ghost and had been my assigned partner and best friend at the MOM since before I could remember . Every monster hunter got a ghost partner because there was no better way of getting secret intelligence than from someone no one else could see or hear. It was a perfect system, most of the time.

Today she was dressed from head to toe in a black ninja outfit and mask, complete with a pair of gleaming silver swords crisscrossing her back. She somersaulted through the bedroom door and over to me, landing in a fierce attack pose, right fist cocked back, ready to strike.

"Uh, why are you dressed like that?" I asked her.

She scanned the room, including the closet overflowing with dirty clothes, and wrinkled her nose. She lowered her fist.

"I thought I heard a girl scream in here."

"Seriously? It sounded like a girl?"

"I'm gonna say it sounded like a nine-year-old, at most. A nine-year-old girl."

"That was me," I told her.

"Oh."

Ruby did a little shake, and her ninja costume and swords vanished, replaced by a pale summer dress and cowboy boots. She looked about fourteen with fire engine red hair, pale skin and a pair of fierce green eyes.

"So what were you screaming about? This closet has looked like this since you moved in."

"You're hilarious, Ruby."

I held out the shredded piece of blue cloth that used to be my Halloween bag.

"What is that?" she asked. "That's not your underwear is it?"

"Look at the teeth marks," I said.

"You have teeth marks in your underwear?"

"No! Just look."

She did, from a distance.

"Okay, and?" she asked finally.

"Don't you get it? Look at those teeth marks! A goblin ate all my Halloween candy."

"Are you serious?" she said. "The dean is gonna freak. That's why you're not supposed to have food in your dorm, Milo."

"He's not gonna freak, and I'll tell you why."

I tossed the shredded Halloween bag on a pile of dirty clothes and bundled it all up into my arms.

"Why is that?"

I tossed the armful of clothes into my room and even Floyd scurried away. I really had to do some laundry, and soon.

"Because, I'm gonna catch the greasy little guy."

I grabbed a piece of chalk from my desk by the bed and sketched out a containment spell on my closet floor. It was a simple rune consisting of a symbol that looked like a single open eye. It was the first spell they taught you here, and it was the most useful.

"We don't have time for this," Ruby said. "That's why I was coming to get you. The dean wants to see us."

"About what?"

I went to my desk and pulled out the bottom drawer, removing it completely. I flipped the drawer over, and there it was. My holdout candy stash. It used to be much bigger, but it had been a rough week, and I had dipped into it pretty regularly. The last chocolate bar was the Peanut Butter Chocolate Explosion, my favourite. I had been saving it for a special occasion, but this would have to do.

Not only was it delicious, but it was said to be made by fast-fingered elves that were like candy making ninjas. All I knew was that by unwrapping the candy, I had rung the dinner bell to any goblins within sniffing distance to Wychwood.

"I don't know. The message just said to go and get you and report to his office."

I peeled away the gold wrapper and instantly my room was filled with the sweet aroma of peanut butter chocolatey goodness. My mouth watered. Even Floyd lifted his head and pawed at me to give him some. Floyd was different from other dogs. I think he was part garbage disposal. He could eat anything. I broke off a piece of the bar and tossed it to him. He snapped it out of the air and swallowed it in one bite. A second later, he was pawing me again.

"Come on, boy, gotta save some for the slimy gobby!"

"Milo, I'm serious," Ruby said. "We have to go."

"This won't take long," I told her.

She shook her head and stared at the digital clock.

"Five minutes and then I'm going without you."

I tied the piece of chocolate to the string that was attached to the closet light fixture. When I was done, the tasty little morsel dangled a good two feet above the closet floor.

I pushed past the clothes hanging on the rod and piled the rest of the dirty clothes on the floor on top of me to both hide me from sight and mask my scent.

"It stinks in here," Ruby said. "I mean, I'm dead, and the smell of your gym socks are making my stomach sick."

I tried to ignore her and the rancid smell of my dirty laundry. This better work, I thought, because I was pretty sure I was going to smell like a laundry hamper for the rest of the day.

Now all I had to do was wait.

"Milo, seriously, we have to …"

Ruby's voice went quiet as green slime rose through the cracks of my closet floor.

CHAPTER THREE

Goblins and all sorts of monsters were categorized into levels. Level threes were the equivalents of grade five kids. They were also not quite completely formed, which meant that a level three goblin was small enough and jelly enough to fit through a keyhole, or even the tiniest crack in the floor.

Wychwood Academy was over three hundred years old and had a ton of cracks. In the walls, in the ceilings and definitely in the floors.

"If this is a level three, you know its catch and release," Ruby told me. "You can't keep a level three."

"I know, Ruby."

We both watched the delicious piece of peanut butter chocolate bar twirl at the end of the light switch string.

The closet floor creaked ever so quietly, and then it groaned.

Slowly, the cracks in the floorboards filled with green slime.

I knew it.

No goblin in the world could resist this chocolate bar.

The slime spread across the floorboards and began to pool into an oozy green puddle. Out of that tiny puddle rose a long hooked nose.

The nose was green, and its wide nostrils flared as it caught a whiff of the peanut butter chocolate delicacy hanging from the string.

My whole body tensed. I didn't breathe, and I didn't speak. I shot a glance at Ruby who looked at the emerging goblin like it was a pail full of cute fluffy puppies.

I shook my head.

Girls.

The goblin gained strength from the goo pushing through the cracks. The nose gave way to a wide mouth full of small sharp little teeth and a large chin. Finally, the goblin's full head popped out. He snapped at the candy on the string, but it was still too high.

The goblin grunted and sighed and, with a wet *thwack,* pulled first his right hand out of the floor, and then his left. His tiny black eyes scanned the closet, sniffing the air, looking for any sign of danger.

Finding none, he pressed down on the floorboards and heaved the lower half of his body through the tiny gap in the wood.

He plopped down, sitting directly on the containment rune I had drawn in chalk.

I stared at the goblin, and I could almost see through him. My clothes on the opposite side of him appeared distorted through the greasy film of his body. He looked like someone had sculpted a chubby ten year old kid out of sixty pounds of green hair gel.

"Awww," Ruby said. "He's so cute."

After a final check around the closet, the goblin reached up, slipped his clawed hand around the piece of candy and yanked down hard.

He was so strong, even at this age, that in his attempt to pull down just the candy, he tore down the string and the light fixture as well. In a single quick snap of his jaws, he tipped back his head and popped every-thing in his mouth in one massive bite. The monster crunched through the plastic and metal of the light fixture. His long forked tongue worked to slurp down the gooey bits of chocolate and peanut butter. He chomped down again and again, not missing an ounce of the sugary goodness.

Gross.

Halfway through, he gagged and spit out the mangled

light fixture in a spray of goo, coating half the clothes in my closet.

Okay, I thought. That was it.

I burst out from under the pile of clothes, pointed at him and screamed, "HA!"

The goblin's black eyes popped open as wide as dinner plates, and his mouth dropped open in a terrified scream. "AHHHHHHHHHH!"

He scrambled to his chubby feet but, before he could get away, I completed the containment spell by saying the final word that made all the magic happen: "Sleep."

The containment rune began to glow a sickly green and, a second later, there was a brilliant flash of green light, followed by a puff of bitter black smoke, which quickly filled the closet and threatened to choke me out. I pushed through the pile of clothes and shoved open my closet door, allowing the plume of offending smoke to filter out into my room.

When the haze cleared, I found a small green glass statue in the centre of the containment rune. I stared at the little face of the trapped goblin.

"What are you going to do with him?" Ruby said.

"I haven't decided yet." I told her.

"You should leave him with the maintenance staff. They'll release him somewhere away from Wychwood."

I told her I would do that and stuffed the glass statue

of the goblin into my pocket as along with the rest of the chocolate bar.

Ruby glanced at the digital clock by my bed, and her face fell.

"What time was our meeting with the dean?" I asked her.

"We are *so* dead," she replied.

CHAPTER FOUR

Luckily the dean's office wasn't far from the senior's dorms. I did nearly bowl over the school librarian, Mrs. Potts, and I'm pretty sure I scared a few freshmen as I ran through the crowded halls screaming, "Run! Run! They're coming!" Just so they would move out of the way. Even Floyd helped with crowd control, barking and yapping as he trotted alongside me, clearing the path as best he could.

I got there right on time. A little sweaty, and definitely out of breath, but on time, nonetheless. I took a second to check myself out in the reflection of a darkened office window. I was a bit taller than most kids in my grade, so I had to slouch in order to see my reflection properly. My short black hair was sticking up in the back, but my usual just-slept-in-my-clothes appearance looked a bit better than normal. I wasn't going to be slicing any onions with the creases in my pants like Toby, but at least this pair looked stain free.

I slammed into one of the three chairs in the dean's waiting room and tried not to stare at his secretary, Elaine Wilks. She was by far the creepiest person on campus—and we had a guy that taught seniors how best to eat snakes, spiders and centipedes if you're ever lost in the Amazon.

Her silver hair was pulled into a bun so severe it looked like it was cutting off the circulation to her head. Her skin was the colour of concrete, and her voice sounded like her throat was filled with broken glass. Her small blue eyes eyed the wall clock as the minute hand ticked toward twelve.

"Eight a.m. Exactly on time," Ms. Wilks rasped. "Mr. Jenkins, I do believe that this is a first for you."

"Yeah," I told her. "I'm turning over a new leaf."

She wrinkled her nose, and her thin smile evaporated. "You should try a new laundry detergent while you're at it. Go on in."

Ms. Wilks may have been the creepiest person on campus, but when it came to Floyd, she lost her freaking mind. Whenever they saw each other, it was nothing but a love fest. Floyd rushed over and leapt up into her lap. Ms. Wilks's grey lifeless face actually developed two small blooms of colour on her cheeks, and she smiled. A real smile, with teeth and everything. I think she nearly pulled her desk drawer off its track trying to get to a dog treat for him.

"Who wants a treat? Who's been a good doggy?" she cooed as she held out the tasty morsel. Floyd, ever the crowd pleaser, stood up on his hind legs to beg for the treat.

"Ooh! Look at you, such a pretty doggy!"

"Weird," Ruby whispered beside me.

"I know, right?"

I crossed Ms. Wilks desk and reached for the door handle to the dean's office. Before I had a chance to turn the knob, the door pulled inward, and standing right in front of me was the dean holding a big beige envelope.

"Well, this is a first. You're on time. You can leave Floyd with Ms. Wilks, as usual."

Apparently, I was developing quite a reputation.

I was about to say something but he raised a hand and cut me off, "There's no time. I'll walk you to the armoury. We've lost too many kids already."

CHAPTER FIVE

The dean didn't have to shout or even speak, the crowds of students in the halls automatically split and hugged the lockers on either side to get out of the man's way. He was an imposing figure to say the least. He was as tall and as wide as an outhouse with arms that were bigger than most people's legs. He always wore a perfectly tailored dark blue suit that wrapped his huge frame from his shiny bald head right down to his polished black shoes.

Another thing about the dean, he walked extremely fast. I had to jog, if not run, just to keep up.

"What do you know about Darius Radish?" he asked me.

I shrugged, stared at Ruby and mouthed, "*Who?*"

"Milo?"

"Uh … Darren …"

"Darius Radish is a Wendigo, sir," Ruby said, saving me. "Extremely greedy breed, they are. He's known for selling illegal weapons to the highest bidder. He broke out of Darkfall Prison a month ago, and no one has seen or heard from him since."

"Until now, Ruby," the dean said. "Three days ago a government scientist, Dr. Stuart Devon, and his eight-year-old daughter, Clare, were taken from his top secret weapons lab in Cripple Creek. From video surveillance, we know that Darius was behind it."

"What was Dr. Devon working on?"

"That we don't know. But if Darius is involved it's probably a weapon. The real problem is every school bus in Cripple Creek has disappeared today, on the way their destinations. Nine buses in total are missing. There's been no contact with the drivers, nothing. Even the GPS units on the buses have gone dark. Only three remain active. We think that whatever Dr. Devon was working on is linked to the disappearing school buses. I need you to get on one of those last three buses and find out what Darius is up to."

The dean handed me the envelope he had been carrying.

"Inside you'll find everything we know about Darius and Dr. Devon."

The envelope wasn't very thick.

Not good.

We had reached the doors to the Wychwood Academy armoury.

CHAPTER SIX

The dean pushed through the frosted double doors and found the lead scientist, Edgar Bodkin standing behind a butcher's block table. He was short with dark hair, darker eyes and grin that always looked like he knew something no one else did. He stood completely still with his hands clasped behind his back. In the near distance machine gun fire echoed, and someone screamed, but the expression on Bodkin's face never changed. A thunderous lion's roar exploded from somewhere to my right, and I jumped in spite of myself. Bodkin and the dean glanced at me as though I was a psycho.

"What was that?" I asked.

"Just a project I'm working on." Bodkin replied matter of factly, "It's not quite ready yet."

"Edgar," the dean said, "I trust everything is in order."

Edgar nodded and gestured to the table of implements. Arranged on the table were a watch, a cell phone, a black hooded sweatshirt and three silver marbles.

"We don't know what you'll be up against, but based on Darius' past terror attacks, we've equipped you with the latest in counter measures.

I stepped to the table and reached for the cell phone.

"Is this the latest mod—"

Edgar slapped my hand before my fingers got near the shiny new phone, and said, "Take off your sweater. Put this one on."

I did as ordered and stood there in the new hoodie. He reached under the table and brought out a spray bottle filled with a purple fluid.

"Recently, Radish has employed chemical warfare ..." Dr. Bodkin said.

"Like at the east Germany Expo," Ruby said.

"Very good, Ruby," Edgar said. " Radish is big fan of poison gas so if you do encounter such a threat—" And he sprayed me with a mist of the purple fluid. It stank of rotting flowers, and suddenly my legs felt like pieces of overcooked spaghetti. The room grew dark, and my vision curled in at the edges. My head spun, but the hood of the sweater extended and slipped over my face, plastering itself to my skin. It joined up with the rest of the sweater to form an airtight seal. Immediately, I tasted a rush of oxygen as the hood converted into a gas mask, flushing out the poison and supplying me with clean, fresh oxygen. My vision came back, and I let go of the counter, able to stand on my feet again. Cameras built into the hood of the sweater allowed me to see and hear everything around me.

So cool!

"You have a limited air supply," Dr. Bodkin said. "Five minutes tops. The hood will activate automatically if it detects gas, but remember the limited air supply. There's a small button on the cuff of the right sleeve; if you push that, you get night vision. But don't push it now."

I pushed it, and everything became so bright I nearly burned my eyeballs out of their sockets. Using night vision goggles in a brightly lit room made it seem like I was staring into the sun.

Dr. Bodkin slipped around the table and double-tapped the button on the cuff, and the hood retracted to become just a simple hood again.

I rubbed my eyes.

"What's with the marbles?" I asked.

"Do you not read any of the gadget memos? Ruby asked.

"These," she said, pointing to the small silver balls, "are

Taser balls. You press opposite sides at once to activate them and, when they contact skin, they send 50,000 volts through that unlucky person."

"Excellent, Ruby," Dr. Bodkin said.

"Teacher's pet," I whispered.

"Just remember not to touch them once they have been activated and, to answer your question, Milo, the phone is, indeed, the latest model with MOM encryption. As is this watch."

Dr. Bodkin flipped open the face of the watch and showed me two small drops of clear gel. "Inside are two tracking gels, they activate on contact and send their locations back to the watch and the phone."

Dr. Bodkin removed the stylus from the phone and, with slight pressure on the end, the writing tip expanded and bristled with keys of all shapes and sizes.

"With new smart gel technology, the stylus is able to pick any known lock."

"Cool."

I slipped the watch over my wrist, and stashed the phone and the magic marbles in my pocket.

"Do try and bring these items back."

"Always," I said.

"In working order," he added.

"No promises, Doc," I told him. "The field can be a dangerous place."

Bodkin fixed me with his dark-eyed shark stare. He was not impressed, and I had no idea what I was running into.

CHAPTER SEVEN

We left the armoury at a dead run. At least, I was running, when I got to the elevator door Ruby was already there waiting for me.

Ding!

The elevator doors parted, and I pushed up stream against the flow of kids exiting the elevator on their way to class. When the last kid left, I pressed my hand to the scanner beside the keypad. My fingerprints were accepted, and a new button materialized on the digital keypad: TRANSIT. I hit it, and the elevator dropped like a stone.

Dr. Bodkin had synced up my watch to show me the GPS locations of the three remaining Cripple Creek buses. Make that two. Two remaining buses.

"Only two left," I told Ruby.

She was getting nervous, and it was more than that scrunched up look she gets on her face. Whenever Ruby got nervous or scared, the air temperature around her dropped. By the time the elevator reached the basement subway system platform, frost covered the elevator walls, and I was shivering.

The subway transit system for Wychwood was unique. Unlike normal subway train cars, the M.O.M. system used smaller, faster egg-shaped pods. These pods were solely powered by electricity and went crazy fast. The system was designed to take MOM agents from Wychwood to any cemetery in North America in a fraction of the time through a system of underground tunnels.

I followed Ruby to our pod, which looked like an egg set on its side. As I approached, the hatch door hissed open. Two people could fit inside, facing each other. I climbed in, strapped myself into the required five point harness and typed in Cripple Creek as our destination on the control panel. The town was small and had only one cemetery, but it was on the north side of town and both remaining buses were in the south.

This was bad.

Ruby still looked nervous, and as soon as she sat down inside the pod, the digital control panel began to develop a thin layer of frost.

"Ruby, you gotta relax," I told her. "You're killing me."

"But those kids," she said. "We're running out of time."

I hit GO and the door to the egg car closed and locked.

I was thrown backward in my seat as the egg rocketed down the tunnel, twisting left and right. We whipped along so fast I could barely see. I loved it.

Ruby said something, but I was only half listening. I just nodded my head as I watched the tunnels whip by the pod window. Riding in these pods was one of my favourite parts of this job. It felt like being shot out of a cannon.

"Are you listening to me?" Ruby asked.

"Yeah," I told her. "Darius Radish. I *had* actually heard of him, in case you were wondering."

"Well, whatever he's selling, the word is that it's something very big." Ruby checked the time on the control tablet. "Where are the last two buses now?"

We continued to rocket down the tunnel, going faster and faster. I checked the status again and saw that only one bus remained on the GPS screen.

One chance.

"There's only one left."

My GPS unit found me the quickest route, but it was still too long.

I wasn't going to make it.

Our pod slowed to a stop and the door hissed open.

"Cripple Creek Municipal Cemetery" was stencilled across the wall in two foot tall faded white letters.

"You have nine minutes before the last kid is picked up, Milo." Ruby told me. "You have to be there before that or they are gone. Doomed."

"I got it, Ruby." I said. "Thanks for the pep talk."

My watch beeped as the countdown started: 00:08:59 ... 00:08:58 ... 00:08:57 ...

CHAPTER EIGHT

I tapped the centre button on my seatbelt and released the straps.

"You got less than nine minutes, Milo," Ruby said. "You have to get to the corner of First and Coventry."

I climbed out of the pod and onto the subway platform. At the far end of the small station, I found the rusted metal exit ladder and climbed to the top. Beside what looked like a manhole cover was a square metal box. I lifted the lid and pressed my hand to the palm scanner. The red light blinked, and then all of the lights glowed green. A second later, the manhole popped open with a hiss. I slid it aside and climbed the rest of the way into the fake tomb that the Ministry of Monsters had built here over one hundred and seventy years ago.

I reset the cover and eased open the tomb door. Rain sliced down as forked lightning clawed at the dark grey morning sky. I zipped up my jacket and slung my backpack over my shoulders.

"Seven minutes and change, Milo."

"Thanks, Ruby." I said glancing at my watch. "I *really* appreciate the countdown."

My GPS said it would take at least nine minutes to get where I was supposed to go. But that was if I followed the regular roads.

I closed the tomb door behind me and headed directly toward the short stone cemetery fence. I jumped up and over and found myself on a gravel road. Rain pelted me like icy darts, and my breath steamed.

Directly across from the cemetery, I ran through a church parking lot and then climbed a chain link fence at the rear of the building into someone's backyard.

My watch still told me to head in that direction so I kept running. I hopped the next fence and, as I landed, my right sneaker squished into a huge pile of dog poop.

Gross.

I pulled my foot out of the stinking pile and wondered what kind of dog poops that big. It was bigger than my backpack.

A second later, a black dog the size of a minivan

exploded out of its weather beaten dog house at the end of the yard and bolted right at me, barking to wake the dead.

Sliding in the poop and the slick grass, I ran until my lungs were on fire. I hit the fence on the opposite side of the yard and scrambled to the top as fast as I could. The crazed, giant dog leapt up after me, growling and snarling and clawing to get at me.

I dropped down onto the other side, water spraying up as my feet hit the ground. I said a quick prayer that there were no more dogs and checked my watch. I had made up some time, but I was still far away.

The air around me got colder. When I looked up, I saw Ruby sitting on the swing set in the back yard. She was dressed like a long distance runner wearing running shorts, high socks and a bright yellow headband.

"Tick, tick, Milo," she said. "Let's go!

Ugh.

I took a deep breath and ran toward the north end of town, passing a Chinese food place, a used car dealership and a boarded up Laundromat. Then I saw it.

First Street.

I checked my watch and kept going west toward Coventry. I rounded the corner of a convenience store and saw the big yellow school bus pulling away from the curb.

"Wait! Wait!" I screamed and waved my hands. I

emptied what little gas I had left in the tank. My legs pumped up and down like pistons as I waved my arms hoping to get the attention of the driver.

I gained some ground and was splashing right alongside it when the brakes on the bus squealed and it pulled over to the side of the road. Hands on my knees I tried to catch my breath as the accordion door folded open.

The bus driver was an aging hippie type sporting a long grey pony tail held back with a bright coloured bandanna. He wore a Hawaiian shirt, cargo shorts and sandals even though summer had been over for months.

"Who're you?" he asked.

"I'm new," I wheezed, still trying to catch my breath. The driving rain had soaked me to the bone but, as I climbed up the first stair, the bus driver held me back with his palm.

"You shouldn't be here," he said.

Despite the cold damp, the bus driver had sweat stains under his arms.. A few tendrils of his grey hair had come loose from the pony tail and stuck to his forehead and cheeks in greasy tangles.

From my angle outside the bus, looking up at the driver's seat, I spotted a black box taped to the underside. Red and blue wires ran from the box up underneath the driver's Hawaiian shirt.

"You don't belong here, son." His voice shook. "I think you made a mistake."

"No," I said, climbing the stairs into the bus. I edged around his seat, trying to ignore what was most likely a bomb. "I'm exactly where I'm supposed to be."

CHAPTER NINE

"There's a bomb under the bus driver's seat." I mumbled under my hand to Ruby.

"What?!" She screamed. "Why are you still on the bus?"

"The whole point of the running through half the town was to get on the bus, remember?"

"Well, at least we know why the buses disappeared." She said exasperated, "They blew up!"

I was barely halfway down the aisle of the crowded school bus when it lurched forward.

I stumbled down the aisle; my arms flailed out and, as the bus made the next right turn, I tripped over something and fell face first into the bus floor.

Kids all around exploded into laughter, and I could feel

my face burning as it turned bright red with embarrassment.

"Smooth move, new kid!" some joker said.

"Don't worry," he continued. "Not everyone saw it." And everyone laughed even louder, especially Ruby. She was back in her student costume, with the black framed glasses slipping to the end of her nose.

I looked and saw that I had tripped over a pad lock that had been attached to the access panel in the floor of the bus.

Who would padlock the access panel?

"Get up, Milo," Ruby said, "Try to be cool."

"I am cool," I hissed.

I slid into an open seat next to a kid studying his iPhone.

"Yeah, super cool," the kid studying his phone said.

Ruby sat across the aisle next to a little kid who clutched a Teenaged Mutant Ninja Turtle lunchbox to his chest.

"Why would anyone put a padlock on the access panel of the bus?"

"Who you talking to?" asked the kid sitting beside me.

"No one." I replied.

"Is that padlock always on the floor like that?"

The kid beside me shrugged and went back to swiping his blank cell phone screen.

"Do you have your phone with you?" he asked.

I pulled my iPhone out of my pocket and handed it to him. It was encrypted by MOM, so I wasn't worried about him seeing anything on there that he shouldn't. The kid tapped the home button, but the screen remained black.

"Yours is dead too." He handed it back.

"What?"

I thumbed the home button again and, sure enough, the phone was dead. A brick.

Dr. Bodkin was gonna kill me if it was busted.

"It had a full charge," I said.

"Same with mine," he said. "I'm Nate."

"Milo."

Nate tapped the boy in front of us in the seat.

"Hey, Jay, does your phone work?"

Jay turned and, through a mouthful of trail mix, he told us it had been working on the street while he was waiting for the bus. After he got on, it went dead.

This wasn't good. Whoever had control of the bus had a way to kill not only our cell signal, but our phones as well.

All around me, the kids studied their blank cell phone screens. Swiping this way and that and shaking their heads. Every cell phone was dead. I checked my watch.

Dead.

Blank.

I was on my own.

Beyond the windows of the bus, the little town of Cripple Creek faded away; we were heading into a warehouse district. We drove for another few minutes turning left and right, getting onto the highway and then exiting onto dirt roads.

With all of their phones dead, the kids looked away from their blank screens and realized something was wrong. The bus slowed and turned right, following the long driveway of a giant, broken down factory. Kids pressed against the bus windows , their eyes wide.

"Where are we?"

"Where's the school?"

"What's happening?"

The bus's front tires rumbled over a pitted parking lot and grumbled toward a large building built like an airplane hangar. The huge doors opened as we approached.

Around me, kids gripped the seat backs in front of them. Some were crying, some were confused, some were still looking down at their dead phones, oblivious.

The bus glided into the hangar, and the solid metal doors closed behind it. Inside the hangar were more busses lined up in perfect rows. I counted eight; every school bus in the town was here. Our bus pulled into the last spot and braked to a gentle stop.

The joker from the front of the bus stood and addressed the bus driver. "What's going on? Where are we?"

A bunch of other students asked the same thing, but the bus driver wouldn't turn around. Probably because he couldn't, due to the bomb under his seat.

"Just relax, kids," the hippie bus driver said weakly staring into the rearview mirror. "Everything is gonna be fine."

The bus beside us was empty. As far as I could tell, they all were.

Where were the other kids?

I looked at Ruby, she looked at me.

"Now what?" I said.

POP!

Everyone jumped as green smoke hissed out from under our seats.

The bus filled with screams as every kid raced into the aisles and charged for the front door. The crush of kids bottlenecked with everyone piling on one another as the accordion door refused to open. There was no escape.

With the main exit jammed, the kids rushed to the windows, yanking and pulling down on the glass partitions as tendrils of the green smoke climbed higher and higher, but every window held fast as if they were welded shut. One hint of gas and my brand new hoody snapped into action, extending and wrapping my face in a tight black mask. I heard a whirring as the power cells and tiny cameras installed inside the hood spun to life. Immediately I felt cool clean air flood over my face. Kids all around me were choking and coughing and slipping to the floor.

I had to get out of here, and fast.

I dove for the access panel and the padlock that I had tripped over earlier. Stampeding kids stomped all around me, climbing over me, freaking out. But it was short lived. The effects of the gas quickly took the fight out of the kids. One minute they were losing their minds, and the next they were dropping like flies, snoring loudly where they fell.

I pulled the stylus from the dead phone, stabbed the pointy end into the lock and clicked the end. I twisted the stylus, and the lock opened easily. With the access panel unlocked I slipped beneath the bus and onto the hangar floor.

I rolled out from under the bus and scrambled to the next one in line.

"Now what?" Ruby asked. At least she was getting into it. She was back in her ninja costume, complete with mask and crossed silver swords.

I had no answer.

For a while, the giant room was silent until a creaking metal door opened at the far end of the hangar. Next came the sound of heavy boots marching toward me.

CHAPTER TEN

Three soldiers all dressed in black camouflage and gas masks pushed flat rolling carts toward the school bus. When they got there, the first soldier pulled a plastic card from his belt and waved it near the door. A moment later, with a series of clicks, the doors and windows of the bus opened, allowing the billowing green smoke to leak out into the huge room.

As soon as I was far enough away from the gas I heard a soft click inside my hoody and the hood retracted from my face.

"I'm gonna go check it out," Ruby whispered.

She rolled out from under the bus and, after taking a running start, did a series of amazing backflips that would have made any ninja proud. Her last backflip ended in a twist and she stuck the landing, right near the first pushcart. She raised her hands in the air and looked back at me. I gave her the thumbs up she was expecting and waited.

One by one, the soldiers carried the kids off the bus and stacked them like pieces of firewood onto the pushcarts.

"They're alive," Ruby said, slipping back beside me under the bus. "I think the gas just knocked them out."

"What do you think they're doing with them?" I asked. She shrugged.

"It doesn't make sense," I told her. "If Darius Radish, the arms dealer, is behind this, what does he want with the kids?"

"We have to get out of here, Milo," she said, "And call MOM for help. This is bigger than I thought."

"You saw where we are. I don't even know where here is. All my electronics were fried when I got on that bus. There's nothing around here for miles, and by the time I find a phone that works ..." I trailed off. "I can't leave them."

I crept up along the bus, getting closer to the front bumper.

"Where are you going?" She asked.

Two of the three pushcarts were loaded to capacity and were being pushed away by two of the soldiers. I watched the last soldier carry my new friend Nate out of the bus and place his limp body onto the pile. The soldier stretched his back before trudging back to the bus and climbing the stairs inside.

Ruby hissed, "Don't!"

But I had a job to do, and I wasn't leaving these kids.

I rolled out from under the bus and, leaving the spinning backflips to Ruby, just ran as fast as I could and jumped onto the last pushcart. I laid face down next to Nate and tried to look asleep.

I waited.

"This is stupid, Milo," Ruby whispered. "Get back to the bus!"

Close by, the bus groaned and squeaked as the soldier stepped down into the hangar.

"Forget that! He's coming! He's coming!"

Next, I heard the stomping of the soldier's boots as they drew closer. I closed my eyes, and a few seconds later, I felt the weight of some other kid being dropped directly onto my back.

Thankfully, the kid was light.

Before I knew it, the wheels of the pushcart began to squeak and squeal as the soldier rolled his load of sleeping kids away from the bus and deeper into the hangar.

CHAPTER ELEVEN

'Playing dead?" Ruby said. "That's your big plan?"

By turning my head slightly to the left, I could just see Ruby sitting on the edge of the pushcart, staring daggers at me. "We should have called for help, but no, you're right … this is much better." Her voice held more than a little sarcasm.

I couldn't risk saying anything. But I wanted to. I *really* wanted to.

"I'm gonna take a look around," she said. "Try to stay alive until I get back, okay?"

I watched her hop off the pushcart and disappear straight through the metal elevator doors.

Ding!

The elevator arrived with a clunk and a wheeze, and

the heavy double doors creaked open. With a grunt, the soldier pushed the cart onto the lift and hit the button for the basement.

We seemed to drop forever until finally the car landed with a thud that made the whole pushcart bounce. One of the kids stacked on the cart farted. And not just a squeaker, this one was loud and wet and smelled like burnt garbage. For a second I thought my hoody gas mask might be activated. Instead, I held my breath as the rotten mayonnaise smell made my eyes water until the elevator doors finally opened.

The soldier gasped as he pushed the cart into another long dark hallway. I guess he was holding his breath too. The hall was lit by a string of portable lights all daisy-chained together along the floor. I couldn't see much, and I wondered if Ruby had found anything interesting.

We ended up in a large room dominated by a strange machine at its centre. Four other hallways, including the one leading back to the elevator, branched off into the darkness of the factory.

Thick cables, pipes and wires snaked away from the central machine that looked like a weird carnival ride with a glass pods arranged around the outside of it. Soldiers carried the sleeping kids and loaded one into each of the glass pods. The glass doors of the pods were then locked on the outside by a metal latch.

All the pods were full except one. The door to that one hung open. The soldier who had pushed my cart all the way down here returned to my cart and grabbed my shoulder.

"Wait," a man's voice hissed, "not that one."

I didn't like his voice. It crawled into my ears like spiders and made my stomach do a little twist.

With a thump, the soldier dropped me back onto the cart and stepped aside.

The air around me grew colder, and I knew that Ruby had returned.

"Uh, oh," she said.

"What do you mean, uh oh?" I whispered.

"It's Darius Radish," she replied. "He told the guard to throw you back on the pile."

"What did you find?"

"I found a way out," she said. "The tunnel directly behind me leads to the sewer. You can get out through a manhole cover."

"Ruby, I can't leave until I know what's going on."

Just then another man's voice tore into the silence of the room. This one was different. Higher and whinier than Radish's. I couldn't see who it was, but he was getting closer and more and more irritated by the second.

"Stop pushing me!" the whiny man said. "I don't understand what I'm doing down here in the first place. I have important work to do! Do you even know who I am?"

I turned my head as slowly as I could and saw Dr. Stuart Devon, the kidnapped scientist, being pushed into the room by two burly soldiers.

"Darius," the scientist whined when he saw the tall man. "We both know I have work to do. What am I doing down here?"

I also got my first glimpse of Darius Radish. To be honest, he was much scarier in person.

The insanely tall man wearing an expensive black suit seemed to materialize out of the gloom. He wore his long, black hair slicked back and small round sunglasses, which did little to hide the burning red bonfires of his eyes.

"For three days you've given me nothing but excuses, Doctor," he said. "So I have found something that might help with your work, as you seem to need a little boost."

"What you're asking for ... it's not possible!" Dr. Devon said. "I really don't think you get that!"

"What you lack is the proper motivation," Darius said. His lips curled into a razor thin smile that revealed a mouthful of sharp, crooked teeth.

Dr. Devon looked confused.

Darius nodded to one of the soldiers, and he disappeared down one of the dark halls branching off of the main room.

"There really isn't a lot of time here, Darius," Dr. Devon said. "The serum will be irreversible in less than an hour."

Darius simply smiled his little smile and said nothing. A moment later, the soldier returned with a young girl in dirty pink pyjamas. Her hair was frizzy and her eyes were red from crying and lack of sleep.

Clare.

"Daddy!" she cried.

Dr. Devon slipped away from the soldiers holding him and bolted toward his daughter.

I didn't even see Darius move. But in an instant the Wendigo was in front of Dr. Devon. With one hand, he lifted the chubby little scientist off his feet. His fingers were incredibly long, as if he had an extra knuckle in there somewhere, long enough that the tips of his fingers and thumb met around the thick neck of the dangling scientist.

Dr. Devon's feet kicked uselessly, as he hung like a fish on a hook from the tall man's arm that never wavered, never grew tired.

"Do you see, Doctor?" Darius said. "I do, *get it*. And I will, *get it*. Do you understand?"

Darius let go of the doctor and he collapsed into a wheezing heap on the cement floor.

"Please," he said. "Don't make her one of

those … things. Time is running out. I won't be able to reverse the effects!"

"Then I suggest you find a way to give me what I want," Darius replied. "Tick tock, doctor."

With a nod from Darius, the soldier picked Clare up off her feet and carried her toward the pod machine in the centre of the room.

"Daddy!" she screamed. "Daddy! Help me! Please!"

Clare was tossed into the last open pod, and the soldier slammed the lid down, locking it with the metal latch.

Immediately Clare slapped her palms against the inside of the glass.

"Please, Darius." Dr. Devon begged. "I'll do whatever you want."

Darius Radish aimed his red eyes at the weeping doctor and said, "Oh, I know you will. And now you'll do it even faster."

Darius gave a signal to a soldier sitting at the computer terminal connected to the machine, and the man tapped the keyboard.

Two soldiers stood on either side of the weeping doctor, propping him up, and facing him toward the machine. Dr. Devon squeezed his eyes shut against the sight.

"Open your eyes, Doctor," Darius hissed. "You don't want to miss this."

CHAPTER TWELVE

The machine grew louder and louder as black sand flowed through the clear plastic tubes running out of the ceiling.

I watched Clare, who had stopped slapping the plexiglass pod and was now staring at the floor. I couldn't see what she was looking at, but whatever it was, she wasn't a big fan. She screamed and climbed higher onto the pod wall, gripping the sides but it was no use. The level of black sand rose higher and higher, filling up the pod like a giant hour glass.

It didn't take long, maybe thirty, forty seconds until the black sand covered Clare completely.

She was buried.

I waited, breathless, until a pale hand slapped weakly against the glass.

The room was still. Everyone's eyes were pinned to the glass pod filled to the top. And then another hand crashed against the inside of the pod, this one was bigger, stronger. And it wasn't just a slap. Whatever hit the inside of the pod was more like a punch and the entire machine shook for a few seconds afterward. The glass pod was actually cracked.

"What was that?" Ruby asked.

The machine slowed its hum, and the sand looked to be lowering. Faster and faster the pod emptied, only it wasn't emptying. It was assembling. The sand was creating something. It looked like. Well, like …

"A monster," Ruby whispered.

Drifts of black sand whirled around the creature that had once been Clare Devon. Though it wore Clare's pink pyjamas, it wasn't Clare. This thing was scaly, dark green and armoured with shiny black dragon scales. Its wide dark green face was dominated by twin eyes that glowed with an eerie green light.

I knew now what the place was. Darius was stealing kids and transforming them into monster soldiers, using Dr. Devon's secret formula.

"What is that? Sand?"

Ruby shook her head, her ninja costume replaced with a white lab coat. She was smiling.

"It's coordinated nano technology."

"It's creepy," I told her.

"It's amazing."

"What happened to Clare?"

"She's still there, but the tiny little nanobots have formed a suit around her."

This place was a monster factory.

The monster formally known as Clare stood incredibly still inside the pod, her arms at her sides. Once the transformation was complete a soldier opened the pod door and stepped back.

Darius smiled and raised his right hand decorated with a large gold ring with a green cat's eye stone.

"Clare," Darius purred. "Do me a favour, and take Dr. Devon back to his lab."

Clare stepped out of the pod and leaped from the machine, landing a few feet from Dr. Devon.

"Clare," he whispered, defeated.

But if his daughter was listening, or understood, she gave no sign. She grabbed him by the elbow and marched him down one of the dark hallways.

"Finish up with this last bunch of kids," Darius told the soldier at the computer terminal, "and then lock this area down. We need to move the machine to the next location."

"Time to go, Milo," Ruby said.

And she was right. I had to move. This was too much.

If I could get to the street, I could find a working phone somewhere and contact MOM and tell them what was going on here.

Out of the corner of my eye, the soldier rose out of his chair. He was coming for me.

"What are you waiting for?" Ruby asked.

I waited until the soldier was close enough I could smell his rotten coffee breath. As he reached for me I snapped my eyes open.

"Boo!" I said, and kicked him square in the nuts.

The big man went down in a wheezing heap, which gave me just enough time to roll off the cart and bolt into the darkness. I activated my hoody again and clicked the button on the cuff. The night vision mode kicked in. The inky dark tunnel began to glow a ghostly green. Everything was clear and as bright as day.

I was halfway down the tunnel, following Ruby, when I heard a bloodcurdling roar.

I did not look back.

Clare was coming for me.

CHAPTER THIRTEEN

Ruby led me to a set of stairs. I grabbed the railing and pulled myself up and up and up. Suddenly something slammed into the stairs, shaking the entire metal frame.

Clare.

Again she roared as her feet stomped up the metal risers.

The exit door was at the top of the next flight, and I emptied the tank to get there. I burst through the door, running full speed, too scared to pay attention to where I was going.

"Milo wait!"

I took two running steps and felt nothing beneath me but air.

I fell through the dark for what seemed like forever and

landed hard on a giant pile of moldy garbage bags filled with what smelled like rotten food and building supplies.

For a second, I thought I might have actually died. I was lying on my back staring up at a hole in the floor. I had fallen straight through it.

"Get up, Milo!" Ruby screamed in my face. "Get up! She's coming!!"

A second later, I saw the monster's green eyes peering down at me from the lip of the hole. It was times like this where I wished my night vision didn't work so well.

I hoped that she couldn't find me in the dark. I closed my eyes and kept perfectly still.

It didn't work.

She dropped down through the same hole I had fallen through. Her armoured feet landed inches from my head. The garbage bags all around me exploded in a gooey wet stink bomb.

Clare reached down and yanked me to my feet. She dragged me all the way back to the machine room where Darius and her dad were waiting.

"Excellent work, Clare," Darius said. "Put him in the pod."

And she did, and not too gently either. Ruby stood helpless beside the pod, looking worried. She had changed back to her summer dress and cowboy boots. It was her favourite outfit, but it did nothing to stop the frost that gathered inside the plexiglass door.

"What do you want me to do?" Ruby asked. "Milo?"

Darius smiled at Clare and fished a treat out of his pocket. It looked and smelled like the dog treats I gave Floyd back at Wychwood.

He tossed it high into the air and Clare's long tongue shot out like a whip and snatched it out of the air, pulling it deep into her throat.

"Gross," I whispered.

Darius patted Clare on the top of the head as he turned away.

"Wait!" I said. "Mr. Radish. I'll make you a deal!"

Darius stopped and tilted his head in my direction.

"You know me?" he said, puzzled.

"That's right," I told him. "You're Darius Radish. You're a Wendigo."

I had his attention now. His full attention. He even took a step back toward the pod.

"A few years ago, you sold the smallpox virus to the Monkey Paw Gang. And you sold the Servants of the Light the Book of Dead Stars."

Even Ruby looked surprised.

"See, I read stuff," I told her.

Darius pulled off his sunglasses, revealing his blood-red eyes. He peered into the pod.

"Do I know you, boy?"

"I know what you're planning to do."

Darius smiled. "Really? And what's that?"

"You're going to sell this machine and Dr. Devon's formula to the highest bidder."

His face fell. His smile gone.

"I've already sent a messenger to the Ministry of Monsters, and they should be here any minute. So, I'll make you a deal. Let all the kids go and run. I'll even give you a head start. Otherwise, I gotta take you down."

A greasy smile spread across Darius's face. It wasn't pleasant. When he spoke next, he sneered, showing me a little snapshot of his fangs.

"Who are you, boy?"

"Jenkins. Milo Jenkins."

Radish smiled and shrugged. "Never heard of you. But you are amusing. Pity you'll be a mindless soldier in a few seconds."

Radish slammed down the cracked pod door and locked it into place.

"Goodbye, Mr. Jerkins," he said.

"It's Jenkins," I told him.

He shook his head.

"Not for long."

CHAPTER FOURTEEN

"No more delays." Darius told the soldier. "We're running out of time; the buyers will be here any moment."

Darius nodded to Clare, who grabbed her father's elbow and once again started led him away.

"Are we suitably motivated, doctor?" Darius asked as they disappeared into the darkness.

I looked at the cracked plexiglass of my pod. I leaned back against the metal frame and kicked it as hard as I could. The glass hurt my foot and didn't give at all. That was never going to work.

"What do you want me to do?" Ruby asked again through the glass.

There had to be a way out. I scanned the inside of the

pod but it was smooth, watertight. There wasn't even a seal. But there was a crack.

"Milo!?"

The machine began to rev up and up, screaming to life, and I knew what that meant. I looked down at my feet and, sure enough, black sand began filling up the bottom of the pod.

"Oh boy."

I searched my pockets for anything I could use and my fingers wrapped around the glass statue of the level three goblin. The sand rose faster now. I climbed up onto the metal framework of the pod and gripped the goblin statue.

"What is that?" Ruby asked, her nose pressed against the glass. "Milo, answer me!"

I squeezed the glass statue of the goblin in my hand asked whoever was listening to please let this work.

"Awake." I said and the glass statue turned to green goo in my fist. The glass melted and dripped onto the metal bed. In a flash, the green goblin reformed into its chubby gelatinous form. Its mouth opened and it squealed and bounced around the inside of the pod. Excited and making weird whooping noises, it dashed from side to side and end to end of the pod.

"You were supposed to give that to the maintenance guys!" Ruby said.

"Not the time, Ruby!"

"Hey! Hey!" I said, and showed the crazed goblin the half eaten chocolate bar I still had in my pocket from this morning. The goblin froze. Its eyes wide as dinner plates.

"You want this?" I asked. It didn't need to answer, I could see the drool dripping from its ghoulish mouth.

"If you want this, I need you to do something for me." I said. "Do you understand?"

The goblin just stared blankly at the chocolate bar.

"Nod your head if you understand me."

Nothing.

The sand was rising, covering the bottom of the metal bed, creeping up over the soles of my shoes.

"Nod your head if you understand me."

Nothing.

"You do something for me or no chocolate. Nod your head if you understand me, or I swear I'll eat this chocolate bar if it's the last thing I ever do! Do you understand me?"

The goblin dropped his head in a quick nod. Once.

Good enough.

"I need you to open this pod door." I said, pointing to the latch lock on the outside of the pod. "Nod if you understand me."

I waved the chocolate bar in front of its face.

The goblin nodded furiously. And then stared at me as the sand crept up over my knee.

"Now," I said.

Still nothing.

"Open the pod now!" I shouted.

The goblin jumped and turned toward the pod door. The sand was past my waist. I estimated I had about twenty seconds before the sand was over my head and I was turned into one of those mindless monsters.

"Come on," I said. "Come on."

CHAPTER FIFTEEN

The goblin placed its hands on either side of the crack in the pod and reared its head way, way back, as far back as its body would allow and then, as hard as he could, the goblin slammed its green jelly head straight at the crack in the glass.

Its head connected with the door with a wet thud that spread its head across the glass like a bug hitting a car windshield at full speed. With its hands on either side of its exploded head, it somehow leaned further forward pushing himself into the crack of the glass pod.

"Hurry, man! Hurry!"

On the other side of the pod door I saw a thin jet of green goo arc onto the floor.

Gross.

Still, the goblin squeezed through the tiny crack like someone was pouring hair gel through a keyhole.

The sand was up to my chest as the green puddle outside the pod reformed into the goblin. Clawed hands reached up from the growing puddle and dragged the rest of its body out of the goo. He stood up, shaking his head and looking confused. For a second, I thought he was going to wander away, forgetting about our deal and why he was even there in the first place. Goblins aren't known for their brain power.

I slapped my hand against the pod door and his tiny black eyes found me. He waved.

I pointed at the metal latch on the outside of the pod as the sand rose past my chin. Still he looked confused. I pointed at the last of my chocolate bar and then back at the latch as the sand covered my face.

I held my breath and plugged my nose, but I didn't hear the lock disengage. I pressed my head against the top of the pod, keeping my face out of the sand as best I could.

Then I heard the smallest, faintest click.

The pod door exploded outward, and the black sand flooded out of the pod, carrying me with it. I tumbled out of the machine and onto the concrete floor in a wave of microscopic nanobots. I was still rolling as a gruff voice yelled, "Hey!" I heard stomping boots and then another rush of black sand as the next pod door sprang open. And the next and the next until all of the doors were flung open wide by the hungry goblin.

Nate, the kid I met on the bus, and the rest of the kids tumbled out of the pods shivering and scared. Rough gloved hands grabbed me by the shoulders and hauled me to my feet.

"What did you do? Get back in there!" the soldier growled.

I reversed his grip on me and snapped a kick toward his knee. I heard the bone crack like dry kindling. The soldier cried out and he collapsed to the floor. His arms pinwheeled as he tried to stay upright, but it didn't help. A half second later, his legs were completely horizontal and he crashed to the cement floor. The back of his bald head knocked against the concrete with a hollow *bong*!

"What's happening?" Nate asked. "How did we get here?"

"That's not really important right now," I told him. "You guys have to get out of here. Fast. Get to the street and call the police."

I pointed toward one of the dark hallways.

"Keep following that hallway till you get to a set of stairs; at the top stay to the right, there's a hole in the floor. After that, there's a sewer exit, which will take you to the street."

Nate stared down into the dark hallway and shook his head.

"It's d-d-d-dark, man. I can barely see in there."

I stripped off my hoody and handed it to him.

"Put it on."

He stared at me.

"Trust me."

Once he had the hoody on, I showed him where the button was on the right cuff. The hood extended and wrapped his face into a killer night vision mask. Nate struggled at first thinking the sweater had come alive and wanted to eat him or something, but he relaxed when the night vision cameras came online.

"Whoa … this is so awesome!"

Nate turned his head left and right. "I can see! I can see in the dark!"

Behind us, the soldier was snorting in his sleep. He wouldn't be out for long.

"Nate," I said, "you need to lead these guys out of here. Can you do that?"

"Sure."

Four of them formed a human chain, holding the hand of the person in front of them as Nate led them down the tunnel. I waited for them to disappear into the dark and then turned to Ruby.

"Now what?" Ruby asked me.

"I need you to go back to Wychwood and get them to send some help."

"What about you?" She said.

"I need to find Dr. Devon. He is the only one who knows how to stop this."

"Then, you're gonna need me right here, because I know where he is."

CHAPTER SIXTEEN

I strolled around the corner and saw the massive guard blocking the lab door. His tree trunk arms were folded across his broad chest. As soon as I stepped one foot into the hallway, his cinderblock head snapped toward me.

"Hey, kid!" he said, as he stomped up the hallway. "What are you doing here?"

"Who? Me?" I said. "I think I'm lost."

He was five feet away.

"Catch." I tossed him one of Dr. Bodkin's silver marbles. Like most people, the giant guard's natural reaction was to catch the little ball and he did. Like a pro. He snatched it right out of the air, and fifty thousand volts blasted through him.

He squealed like a scared little piglet, crumpled and fell face down onto the floor.

I ran up to the giant and snatched the magnetic key card from his belt. I swiped it across the access panel and the lab door slid open.

Inside the doctor's lab was a high-tech ring of computer equipment and high definition screens. Against the far wall were stacks of bent and broken animal cages. It smelled like a petting zoo. Some of the cages were covered in goo and fur.

Dr. Devon's head rose from his computer desk, where it looked like he had been crying. If it was possible, he actually looked worse than the last time I saw him in the machine room. His eyes were bloodshot and his skin looked grey. What remained of his brown hair stuck up straight from his shiny scalp.

"Who are you?" he asked me. "What is this?"

He made his way around the computer station, his white lab coat flapping behind him.

"What have you done?"

The guard at my feet was waking up, and when he did, he would not be happy.

"I need your help," I told him, "Now! Before this guy wakes up."

The doctor ran to the door and grabbed the soldier's feet. Together we dragged the big guy into the lab, straight across the floor and into one of the bent and broken monkey cages.

With the soldier locked safely away, I turned to the good doctor.

"Hi, I'm Milo," I said. "I'm here to save you."

A faint smile flickered across the tired looking doctor's face.

"What are you doing here? When they realize the guard is not out there in the hall they're gonna come in here and kill us both."

He pointed at me.

"Wait, I know you. You're the boy from downstairs. How did you get out of the pod?"

"That's a long story," I told him. "We gotta go. Come on."

"I can't go," he said. "Not without Clare."

Yeah, Clare. The monster that chased me and was now a lapdog to Darius.

"That might be a problem."

"My Clare is gone. Transformed into one of those things. One of those things I made. She's lost forever in …" He checked his watch. "Eleven minutes."

"What do you mean?"

"The black sand, the monster serum is actually made up of billions of tiny nanocomputers that, when directed, assemble and create a monster soldier suit of armour."

"I told you." Ruby said, wearing her white lab coat and holding a clipboard for some reason.

"Completely without fear, without remorse. Controlled by a ring that I designed. The serum takes hold completely after seven hours."

"What do you mean takes hold completely?"

"Each batch of serum has a shelf life of seven hours. It can be turned on and off during the seven hours, but after seven hours, the serum attaches itself to the host, and it becomes permanent. No matter if you come into contact thirty seconds after the serum is activated, or thirty seconds before the seven hour period. After seven hours the serum and the host are forever linked. It's one of the many flaws that I was working on when Darius kidnapped us."

"So Clare and all those kids will …"

"Be mindless monster soldiers forever," the doctor said.

"How do we reverse it?"

"I can issue the nanobots a kill code before the seven hour deadline and reverse the effects of the monster serum. But I need the controller ring, and Darius has it."

Awesome.

"It's pointless. She's doomed. We're all doomed," the doctor whined.

"Down in the machine room, he said he would turn Clare back to normal if you gave him what he wanted."

"What he wants is impossible."

"What is it?"

"I call it SPF. It's my super performance formula, SPF. The first monster serum creates a suit around the subject. The SPF is not a suit you wear. The formula changes you. It modifies your cells into something … better, stronger, faster. But it doesn't work."

"What does it do?"

"It's supposed to turn the specimen into an ultra-monster. Bigger, stronger, faster than all the rest," he said. "In theory. One super monster would be more powerful than fifty of the normal ones. I've been working on it forever, but it doesn't work. Just look."

The doctor waved a hand at the array of cages lined along the wall behind him. The twisted metal bars, the dripping goo, the charred cage.

"The test subjects, so far, every one. Every single one. Gorilla, goat, dog, monkey. They've all exploded under the stress of the formula."

"Exploded?" I said.

"You're not doing that." Ruby crossed her arms. "I was wrong. This guy isn't brilliant, he's a dangerous maniac."

"I tried to tell Darius this whole time. I haven't figured it out yet. The subject is injected with the serum, it starts doing what it's supposed to and then … *SPLAT!* They explode. It's as simple as that."

"Have you tried it with a human subject?"

"Are you insane?" he said. "Absolutely not. Besides, no one is really jumping at the chance to be the guinea pig after the gorilla exploded."

"Fair enough."

The doctor was right, those kids were doomed.

———————

CHAPTER SEVENTEEN

———————

Dr. Devon looked at his watch again. "Nine minutes. The only way to get that kill code to the nanobots is to access the software, and I can't do that without the ring Darius wears. Without it, it's useless."

I stepped to the doctor's computer station and eyed a giant needle capped with a piece of cork. "Is this the SPF?"

The inside of the glass fronted syringe gave me a clear view of the liquid inside. It was moving, like a blue swirling hurricane inside the glass.

"Don't even think about it, kid." the doctor warned.

"Why does it do that? Swirl like that?" I asked.

"It's complicated," he said. "Still, it doesn't work, unless you want to explode something."

The air around me cooled as Ruby slipped between me and the serum.

"You stay here with the doctor and hide. I'll go get help from MOM," Ruby said. "Don't do this."

"Don't do what?"

"Are you talking to me?" the doctor asked.

"I know you." Ruby looked hard at me.

If we waited until the timer clicked down to zero, Clare and all of those kids were doomed. If I tried the serum, I could explode.

"There's no time," I said.

"In this job, you win some and you lose some, Milo," she said. "You can't save everyone."

"Maybe not," I told her.

I moved toward it.

"What are you doing?" the doctor asked.

I ignored him. "I know what I'm doing," I told Ruby.

"No you don't," Ruby said. "You're going to get exploded like the monkeys."

"The nanomachines were programmed to operate in humans, not monkeys, right doc?"

The doctor wriggled his face and shrugged his shoulders as he moaned out a, "Yeah, but … still …"

"See?" I told Ruby. "Piece of cake. They just stopped testing the serum because it blew up the monkeys."

Dr. Devon looked around to see who I was talking to.

"And the goats," the doctor chimed in. "And gorillas."

"Whatever, Doc," I snapped. "The point is, they never tested the serum on its intended subject."

I grabbed the syringe and held it in my right hand. It was a lot heavier than I thought it would be. The metal of the needle was freezing.

"How much time left?" I asked the doctor.

"Eight minutes and change."

I uncapped the syringe and stared at the shining tip of the syringe.

Ruby said, "Oh my God. This is the end."

The room dropped into a deep freeze as Ruby freaked out.

The doctor rubbed his shoulders, and when he spoke, his breath clouded in front of his face.

"What's happening?" he asked. "Why is it so cold in here?"

"It's gonna work." I said a little breathlessly, more to myself than anyone else. "Just relax."

I started to sweat. Wow, I really hated needles. Like, a lot. This was a mistake, I thought. Ruby and the doc were right. I'm gonna explode all over this secret lab.

I looked at the clock, less than eight minutes now before all those kids were transformed into monsters forever.

No choice.

No time to wait.

I slammed the needle into my thigh and pushed the plunger.

CHAPTER EIGHTEEN

hoa!

Instantly I could feel the stream of miniature nanomachines swarm through my leg in a freezing cold tide. I looked down and the syringe was empty. I pulled the needle from my leg and let it clatter to the floor. Feeling spent, I slumped back into a rolling desk chair.

"Wow," I said. "That hurt a lot more than I thought it would."

Dr. Devon took a nervous step back, and Ruby did the same.

"How do you feel?" the doctor asked.

I thought about it. The pain in my thigh where the giant needle went in was fading ,and my leg actually felt a little numb.

"Fine, I guess?"

Then it happened.

My leg started tingling, like pins and needles, until every muscle in my leg seemed to pull and stretch at once. I heard a loud *riiiiiip!* as my leg suddenly grew five, six times its normal size and stretched right through the leg of my jeans!

My bare right leg was entirely blue. My once scrawny legs were covered in thick cables of muscle and veins as wide as my finger. There was another big rip as my right foot tore straight through my sneaker and sock. Shredded pieces of rubber, leather and cloth flew toward the doc and Ruby.

I'm not ashamed to say it. I screamed.

A lot.

And very loudly.

When I could breathe again I asked, "Is this ... normal?"

The doctor's mouth hung open as he shook his head. "I've never gotten this far before. They ... usually explode by now."

Soon my other leg began to tingle and then—

Boom!

It too ripped through my jeans and my shoes. The weight and size of my new legs smashed through the desk chair, and I toppled to the ground with a thud.

I scrambled to my feet and found I was nearly nine feet tall. My head, my still normal head, was scraping the ceiling tiles.

"Is this it?" I screamed. "I get blue monster legs?"

Dr. Devon and Ruby couldn't stop staring, their jaws by their knees, just about. Clearly they had no answers for me.

Well, maybe I could kick the ring off of Darius, I thought.

I took a step toward the door; the massive guard was curled up against the bars of the monkey cage, his eye open. He laughed when he saw my legs.

This was a nightmare.

Just then, my stomach felt like someone had stabbed me with a hot poker, and I doubled over. My insides rolled around my belly. I heaved and heaved like I was going to puke, but the urge passed.

What was happening now?

I opened my mouth to ask for a glass of water or a bucket to puke into when instead of my normal, albeit tiny voice, a new monsters roar thundered out of my throat. New sharp teeth pushed their way out of my gums. My hands curled into fists and slammed into the ground, shattering the tile floor. Bulging muscles twisted around my arms ending in my gigantic blue hands, tipped with black razor sharp claws.

I heard a whimper. The muscled guard wasn't laughing anymore.

I turned toward him and roared! Flecks of spittle splashed against the bars and the guard's face as I roared louder than any lion on earth. The not-so-giant guard scurried to the far end of the monkey cage, sniveling in fear.

Awesome.

I stood to my full height, and my head punched through the ceiling tiles. I bent a little lower so I could find the doctor, who was cowering behind his computer terminal.

My voice was deep and sounded like my throat was filled with gravel. "Where's Darius?"

CHAPTER NINETEEN

I followed Ruby, dressed like an elite army commando going into battle, as she lead me through the twisting hallways of the building. Dr. Devon ran behind, carrying his laptop.

She pointed at a double wide steel door, and I ran full blast, roaring as I went. I lowered my shoulder and gritted my new monster teeth and slammed every ounce of my weight right into it.

And bounced right back.

Darn.

I made a dent, though. I rubbed my shoulder and got back to my feet.

"It's a pull, Milo," Ruby said. "Not a push."

I saw the door handles and gently pulled one toward me. The door opened easily.

"Don't worry," Ruby said, "if you make it back to Wychwood, I won't tell everyone about that." She was trying really hard not to laugh.

"Six minutes, Milo," Dr. Devon said. "We have to hurry."

Inside the hangar, Darius stood in front of at least five hundred monster soldiers, arranged in a neat formation. I squeezed through the doorway and stepped inside.

"You see, this proves my point," Darius said. "With the proper motivation anything is possible."

He stared at me as I walked across the hangar floor.

"Look at that musculature!" Darius said. "Amazing!"

Dr. Devon stuck close to the wall, his laptop clutched to his chest.

"Congratulations, Doctor. Well done."

"I want my daughter, Darius," Dr. Devon told him. "I want Clare."

"Well, we all want something, don't we, Doctor."

"All I want is your ring." I growled.

"What? This ring?" Darius said, wriggling the gold controller ring, which spun wildly around his grey pinky finger.

"That's the one," I told him.

Darius looked to his platoon of monsters standing at attention. They were fixated on me now. Black armoured skin rippled with muscles. Glowing green cat's eyes focused on nothing but me.

"You really wanna go down that road?" he asked me.

I nodded, trying to look a lot more confident than I felt.

"Then come and get it," he said with a sneer.

Darius held up his controller ring, and said, "Stop him."

The monsters did not hesitate. They rushed me all at once and all together. Roaring wildly with their claws outstretched. They came in a hideous tide of black flesh and razored fingernails.

I looked around for something to use as a weapon and grabbed the bumper of one of the nearby buses. With a squeal of ripping metal, it yanked free. Igripped it like a baseball bat.

"Come on and get some!" I screamed and took a big baseball swing at the first wave of unlucky monsters.

Black leathery bodies flew everywhere, tumbling through the air and shrieking as they went. But more were coming. I drew back the bumper and took another big swing. More monsters flew to the left and right, pinwheeling through the air. I kept my eyes on Darius as he began to move toward the opposite end of the hangar.

I stomped through the crowd of monsters. They attacked my legs now, grabbing on tight and holding me. I tried to shake them off, but every time I removed one, two took its place. And they kept coming.

And what was worse, the tingling was coming back to my legs. The blue tint to my skin was fading back into my normal skim milk complexion. The SPF had run its course, and I was fading into my old self.

I stomped faster, shuffling my feet, but the monsters crawled all over me. Wrapping themselves around my legs, climbing over my body and hanging off my arms. Biting and clawing and scratching me. My legs were shrinking and the monsters were piling on.

I took another step toward Darius, reaching out my massive right claw, but then I was falling. Crashing into the concrete floor. I was able to look up for a moment, but I could feel the monsters holding me down, pressing my face into the ground. I was turning back into myself, and I just wasn't strong enough to hold them off any longer.

From under the dog pile of monsters, I heard Darius's voice.

"Well, that was exciting." And then, "Stand him up."

The super performance formula was well beyond wearing off. My body had shrunk and shrivelled to its pre-SPF serum size. Rags of my clothes still clung to me but I was in a lot of danger of being completely naked if I moved too quickly. I still felt weird, tingling throughout my whole body, and I wondered what the nano machines had done to my insides and if there would be any lasting effects.

The monsters lifted and dragged me to my knees, where they could control me. They only needed one on each side with their talons poking into my biceps.

Darius tilted his head as he looked at me and smiled.

"Mr. Jerkins, we meet again. You got a lot of heart kid. But sometimes heart isn't enough. You gotta be smart. And this, trying to beat all my monsters at once, just isn't that smart. Obviously."

"I wasn't trying to beat them all."

"Well, that's good," he told me.

"I just needed to get close."

Darius squinted his burning red eyes at me.

"Close enough to do what?"

"This." I told him. "*Sleep*."

He had time to ask, "What did you say?"

And then it was too late.

While I was under the dog pile of Darius's monster soldiers, I used my razor sharp fingernails to scratch a containment rune into the concrete floor. With a single word, the spell I had carved began to glow a bright white. The floor around the trapped Wendigo erupted in a flash of blinding white flame.

Darius turned and tried to bolt away, but he was trapped. He twisted and squirmed, but it was no use. He screamed and clawed at the light keeping him prisoner, but he was already shrinking, being condensed by the power of the rune into one tiny white glass statue. A moment later, there was a flash of white light, and he was gone in a puff of smoke. All that remained were his clothes, his shoes and one monster soldier controlling ring lying on the floor in a pile.

CHAPTER TWENTY

With the ring unattended the monsters were stuck, frozen in their last command. I wriggled away from the two holding me and scooped up the ring.

"Doc!" I screamed. "Doctor Devon!"

The doc raced over and we met in the middle of the hangar.

The doctor opened his laptop, and I handed him the ring. A timer was counting down in the top right corner of the computer. The seconds ticked by so fast I could barely see it.

The doctor grabbed the ring and slipped it into place on the frame of the laptop. The ring was locked into the computer and the entire console began to glow.

"Come on, come on!" the doctor whispered, watching the countdown …

00:00:11 … 00:00:10 … 00:00:09 …

Finally the screen beeped, and the doctor's fingers flew over the keys.

00:00:03 … 00:00:02 … 00:00:01 …

"Done!" he shouted and rocked back on his knees away from the computer.

I looked to my left and then to my right. The monsters stared back at me.

"Nothing is happening!" I said.

The timer on the screen flashed red and stayed that way, blaring a giant warning message across the screen:

SUPER SOLDIER SERUM: LOCKED

The doctor looked at the screen, his hands pulling at what little hair remained on his balding head.

"No! That's not right! It can't be!"

The doctor screamed and began attacking the keys again, flicking his bulging eyes up at the frozen monsters behind me hoping for something to happen.

"This isn't right! This can't be, please, no! No! NO!"

The doctor finally slammed the laptop shut and dropped to the concrete floor weeping. He was really crying, wailing, "Clare! Clare!"

And then I heard it.

It was loud and long and sounded like a burp.

"Was that a burp?" Ruby asked.

Dr. Devon looked up from where he lay on the floor, his red eyes fixed on a monster stumbling away from the pack.

As we watched the monster took another lurching step and dropped to one knee. He was wearing a Hawaiian shirt and cargo shorts and his monster hands were laced over his belly. He dropped to the ground on all fours and let out an even louder burp. He made some dry heaving sounds, and I knew what was coming. I ran back to the pile of Darius's clothes and scooped up the glass statue of Darius Radish and ran back to the doc.

"We gotta get out of here."

"What? Why?" he asked. "What's happening?"

Before I could answer, the first monster burped again and its mouth opened like one of those old Pez flip top candy containers and a viscous stream of black sand exploded out of his throat.

"Oh, wow," the doctor said, as I pulled him backward toward the buses. "Oh, wow."

Now the second monster was throwing up. And then a third and a fourth until every monster in the hangar was puking their guts out on the concrete floor.

The more they threw up, the more the kids and teachers and bus drivers started to look like themselves.

Dr. Devon pulled away from me and pushed his way into the puking crowd.

"Help me find her!" he said. "Help me find Clare!"

I ran along the edge of the crowd until I spotted the monster wearing the pink pyjamas. Dr. Devon was already there, rubbing his daughter's back as she tossed up the last of her daddy's invention and returned to her normal self.

I found the switch to open the huge hangar doors and could already hear the sirens of emergency crews racing to our location. Police cars, ambulances and even fire engines were screaming across the pitted parking lot.

I guess Nate had made it to the sewer exit after all.

Ruby was out there too, speaking to a familiar large blonde woman in a flower-patterned dress. She was a ghost, just like Ruby. The edges of her hair and body were blurry, as if she were made of smoke. The woman said something confidential to Ruby, leaning in close and whispering it into her ear, and Ruby smiled. I wondered what she said.

A moment later, amid the chaos of the arriving emergency crews, Ruby drifted back over to me, a smile lifting the corners of her mouth.

"Ms. Wibberly wanted to let you know that you did a good job today, Milo," Ruby said.

Ms. Wibberly, that's who she was—the professor of wraiths at Wychwood. I knew I'd recognized her.

"You see, everything worked out all right," I told her.

Ruby dropped down beside me against the tire of a school bus.

"Well, injecting yourself with untested monster serum was, overall, super stupid, and I can't believe it actually worked. But … yeah. You beat the monsters, you saved the girl and you didn't die. Job well done."

I stared over at the spot where Ms. Wibberly had been standing, but she was gone.

"What was Ms. Wibberly doing here, anyway?"

"She told me the dean wants us to check on something before heading back to Wychwood. Apparently there's a Sasquatch causing some problems north of Seattle."

I got to my feet and looked down at my shredded clothes. Everything had been ripped apart except my underwear, which were hanging on by a thread.

"There is no way I can go to Seattle like this."

"Why? You look fine." She said.

"How does this look fine?" I said, wrapping the tattered remains of my pants around my waist.

Ruby shrugged and stepped toward the road.

"Orders are orders, soldier, and the dean wants us there, pronto."

How was I supposed to fight a Sasquatch in my underwear? I glanced around; maybe someone left an extra change of clothes on one of the buses. Even a pair of shoes would have been nice. It was freezing outside.

"You gotta help me find some new clothes," I called after her, but she was already gone.

I looked left and right. She just disappeared, and I realized that I had no idea where I was or how to get back to the cemetery.

"Ruby?"

I stepped out into the parking lot and spied the red tangle of her hair as she slipped through the chain-link fence. I gripped what amounted to a jean skirt tight around my waist and raced to catch up to her, and I swear I could hear her laughing in the distance.

"Ruby wait!"

If you have enjoyed Monster Factory I would really appreciate it if you took the time to leave an honest review. Thanks for reading and as always, stay safe and take care!

Milo and Ruby will return in
The Blackwell Witch.

ABOUT THE AUTHOR

Patrick McNulty has been fascinated with monsters and twisted stories his entire life. He is an author, screenwriter and father to three amazing children. He lives in southern Ontario, Canada with his family and a dog named, Charlie.

9 781999 531201